This book belongs to

....

How this collection works

This collection offers six funny and engaging stories for your child to enjoy reading. They are specially written to support and develop your child's growing reading skills, and give your child plenty of opportunities to practise their phonic skills and develop their reading comprehension.

Reading should be a shared and enjoyable experience for both you and your child. Pick a time when your child is not distracted by other things, and when they are happy to concentrate for about 15 minutes. Just one of the stories in this collection is about the right length for a reading session.

Tips for reading the stories together

Step 1 – Look together at the title page for each story before your child starts to read. What does your child think the story will be about? Use clues from the title and picture and talk about what might happen.

Step 2 — Ask your child to read the story out loud. Encourage them to stop and look at the pictures, and talk about what they are reading — either during the reading session, or afterwards. Your child will be able to read most of the words in the story, but if they struggle with a word, remind them to say the sounds in the word from left to right and then blend the sounds together to read the word, e.g. *d-r-ea-m, dream*. If they come across a tricky word that they cannot sound out, simply read the word to your child, e.g. *I, the, no.*

Step 3 — When your child has finished reading the story, discuss it together. Then turn to the fun activities at the end. These will help your child think and talk about what they have read.

Contents

OXFORD
UNIVERSITY PRESS

SnoOt's Big Bad Dream

Written by

Simon Puttock

Illustrated by

Thomas Docherty

Every morning, Snoot
woke up feeling worried.

"What if the sky falls down?" said Snoot.

"What if I step on a
crack in the pavement?"

"Oh dear," said Snoot. "What if two stripes aren't *enough*?"

"What if something terrible happens?"

"Snoot," said his friend Milton, "you worry too much."

But one night, something terrible *did* happen.
Something terrible tapped at Snoot's bedroom door.

"Snoot!" it boomed.

"I'm your **big bad** dream and I am going to **get** you!"

Snoot hid under
the covers all night.

"Dreams can't *hurt* you, Snoot," said Milton.

"But Milton, it was terrible," said Snoot. "And horrible. And dreadful, too!"

"If it comes back, you must chase it away," said Milton.

"I can't do that," said Snoot. "It's too scary!"

The next night, the big bad dream was waiting at the top of the stairs.

"Snoot!" it boomed.

"I am going to get you!"

Snoot hid in the downstairs bathroom until morning.

"Next time," said Milton, "say this. *Go away, you big bad dream and do not dare come back again!* That should do the trick."

"Oh!" cried Snoot. "I can't say that! I'm not brave enough."

That night, Snoot was about to eat his tea
when the big bad dream came creeping in.

"Snoot!" it boomed.

"I am going to **get** you!"

Snoot didn't stop running until he got to Milton's house.

"Snoot," said Milton sternly. "You **must** make this dream go away. If you don't, you will be stuck with it forever!"

"Forever?" howled Snoot. "Oh no!"

"Don't worry," said Milton. "Next time I will **help** you to be brave."

That night, the big bad dream came creeping in once again.

Then the big bad dream saw Milton.

"*Yikes!*" said Milton, and he hid behind the sofa.

But Snoot did not say "yikes".
Snoot did not hide behind the sofa.
Suddenly, Snoot felt very cross.

"How *dare* you scare my friend like that!"
Snoot shouted. "You're not *Milton's* dream!
You are *my dream* and
      I will not let you scare him."

Just like that, the dream began to shrink!

"And because you are *my* dream, you will do what
I say!" said Snoot.

The dream shrank a bit more.

"And *I* say, **go away**,
you big bad dream
and do not dare
come back again!"

Snoot's dream shrank to the size of a potato.

In a tiny voice it said, "I'm really very sorry."
And then it vanished.

"Snoot," said Milton, "you bravely *saved* me!"

"Yes!" said Snoot happily.
"I suppose I *did!*"

When Snoot woke
up the next morning,
he felt different.

He did not feel worried, he felt good.

"Hello," he said to himself in the mirror. "I like your stripes!"

The Snoot in the mirror grinned back at him.

It was raining.

"Goodness, the sky *is* falling," Snoot thought.
"I shall need an umbrella."

Then he went out and stepped on a pavement crack ...

... and guess what?

Nothing terrible
happened at all!

Talk about it!

How did the big bad dream make me feel at first?

What happened when I got cross with the dream?

Do you think I will have problems with that dream again? Why, or why not?

Scaring the bad dream away

What is Snoot's bad dream thinking?
Write it in the thought bubble.

Have you ever had a bad dream?
Draw yourself frightening the bad dream away.

How the Bink Got Its Stink

Written by
Jeanne Willis

Illustrated by
Tony Ross

Once, there was a family of Binks.
There was Father Bink,

Mother Bink,

Sister Bink

and Brother Bink.

They were the only Binks
left in the woods.

Mother Bink was about
to have twins.

But *something* was out to get them.

The Binks were very sweet and soft.
They were too sweet and too soft for
their own good.

They had no teeth to bite with.

And no claws to fight with.

One day, Sister Bink met a Snappy Fang.
"Hello, good to meet you!" said Sister Bink.

"Good to eat you!" said the Snappy
Fang. And he gobbled her up.

Gobble!
Gobble!

"Yum! So soft, so sweet!" said the Snappy Fang.
"Binks are easy to eat. No teeth to bite me and
no claws to fight me."

When Sister Bink did not come home,
Brother Bink went to look for her.

On the way, he met the Snappy Fang.
"Hello, good to meet you," said Brother Bink.

"Good to **eat** you!" said the Snappy Fang.

And he gobbled up Brother Bink.

Gobble!
Gobble!

"Yum. So soft,
so sweet!" he said.

38

"Binks are easy to eat. No teeth to bite me and no claws to fight me. But I am still hungry!"

So he hid and he waited.

Father Bink went to look for his children.
The Snappy Fang saw him and jumped out.

"Hello," said Father Bink.
"Good to meet you!"

"Good to eat you!" said the Snappy Fang.

And he gobbled up Father Bink.

Gobble!
Gobble!

"Yum. So soft, so sweet!" he said.

"Binks are easy to eat. No teeth to bite me and no claws to fight me. I will catch another one!" said the Snappy Fang.

He hid and he waited.

Father Bink, Brother Bink and Sister Bink
had not come home.

"Where are they?" said Mother Bink.

There was a knock at the door.

But it was not them.

It was the Wise Old Woodman. He had seen
the Snappy Fang eat the Binks and he was sad.
Soon there would be no Binks left in the woods.

"Mother Bink, I cannot make you less soft or sweet," said the Wise Old Woodman.

"I cannot give you teeth to bite or claws to fight. But I do have a way to save you and your babies, when they are born."

He made a special stinky cream and gave
it to Mother Bink.

"That will do the trick," he said.

Mother Bink put it on her fur.

Squirt, squirt!

The next day, Mother Bink had her baby twins.
She put the cream on their fur, and she took
them out to show them off.

When the Snappy Fang saw them, he licked his lips.
"Yum! *Three* Binks!" he said. "One for breakfast, one for lunch and one for tea!"

And he jumped out.

Rarrrrrrr!

"Hello, do you want to meet my babies?" said Mother Bink.

"I want to **eat** your babies!" said
the Snappy Fang.

But as the Snappy Fang looked into the pram …

... he smelled the **stinkiest** stink that ever stunk.

"Yuck! Binks are smelly! I don't want them in my belly!" said the Snappy Fang. "I would rather starve than eat one."

He hiccupped and out came all the Binks!

That is why there are still Binks in the woods.

And that is how they got their stink!

Talk about it!

Why was I so keen on eating the Binks?

What useful thing did the woodman give Mother Bink?

What happened to Father Bink and the children in the end?

Join the rhymes

Draw lines to join the rhyming words.

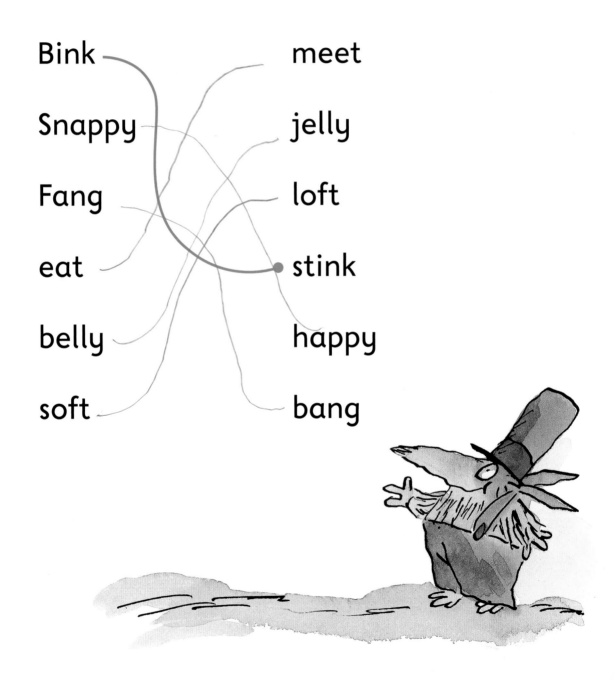

Bink   meet

Snappy   jelly

Fang   loft

eat   stink

belly   happy

soft   bang

My Sabre-tooth Pet

Written by
Aleesah Darlison

Illustrated by
Ben Whitehouse

Hi. My name is Fleet. This is the story of my pet. He's a sabre-tooth kitten called Smiley.

All my friends have pets. Grub has
a cave bear called Odo. Odo is cute
but he can cause problems!

Grub's sister, Daisy, has a pet sloth called Huggle.
He loves to cuddle and sleep all the time.

Even Link, the really mean boy,
has a pet. His wolf is called Kruncher.
Kruncher growls and dribbles a lot.

Link does not like Smiley.

"That fluffy kitten's not a real pet, like Kruncher!"

I don't care what Link thinks. I know
Smiley is the best pet.

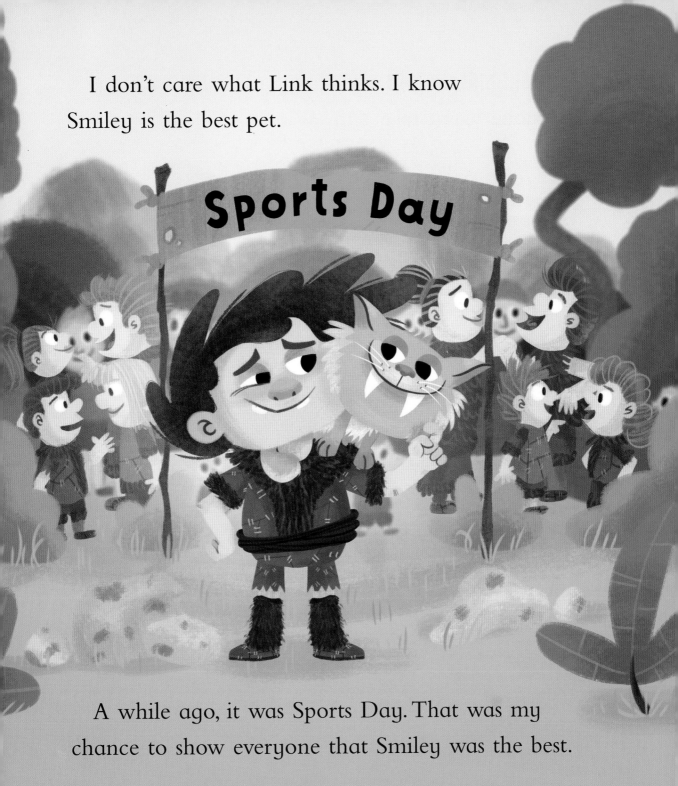

A while ago, it was Sports Day. That was my
chance to show everyone that Smiley was the best.

All the children and pets take part in Sports Day.
Everyone wants to get the Winner's Shield.

On Sports Day, we had to do the obstacle course first.

The obstacle course looked *really* hard!

"This will be so easy," grinned Link.

Smiley and I had a go at the obstacle course.
We were doing well until we got to the mud pool.
Smiley doesn't like mud. He hates getting his
fur dirty.

But Smiley didn't want to do it.

Grub and Daisy were finding it hard, too.

We didn't even finish the obstacle course.
Link and Kruncher did well though.

"Bad luck, Fleet," Link said in his meanest voice.

The next event was canoeing.
It's hard to go canoeing in
a river full of crocodiles!

Smiley and I tried our best but the
canoeing event was too hard for us.

We ended up in a bit of trouble.

Grub to the rescue!

Luckily, Grub spotted us.

Link and Kruncher didn't have any trouble with the crocodiles.

They won the canoeing event, too!

"Don't worry, Fleet," said Daisy.

But Sports Day was harder than I thought.

What if Smiley wasn't the best pet after all?

"Link and Kruncher are winning everything,"
I groaned.

The mammoth chase was the last event, and the hardest event. You had to chase the most mammoths across the finish line to win.

But this was our last chance to win something. We had to try.

As soon as we set off, there was a problem.
Instead of us chasing the mammoths, they chased *us*!
The sound of thundering mammoths
filled the air.

I was really scared.
"Run away, Smiley!" I shouted.

But Smiley wouldn't leave.
He stood still and let
out a mighty

ROAR!

He made a lot of noise, for a tiny kitten!

When Smiley roared, all the mammoths ran away.
Smiley had saved the day!

"That was close. You saved us all, Smiley," said Link.
"Thanks, Smiley!" said Grub and Daisy.

We didn't get the Winner's Shield but Smiley got
a better prize. It was the Bravest Pet award!

After our big day, I did some drawings in
our cave. I wanted people to remember the
story of Sports Day forever.

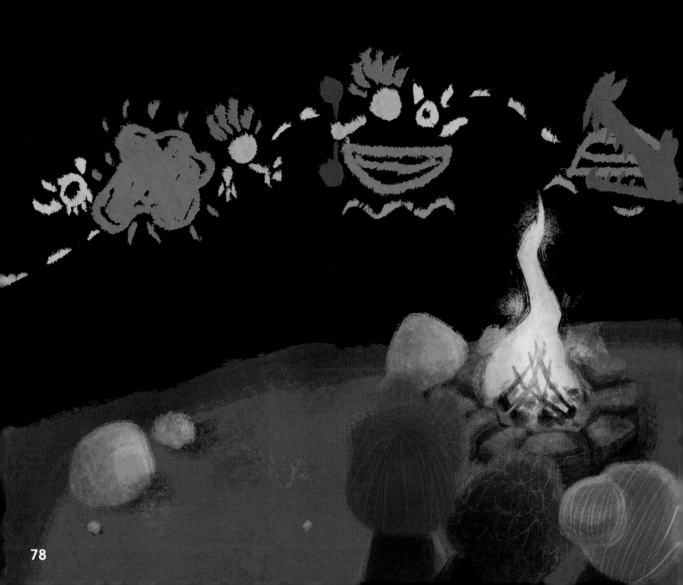

So now everyone will know the truth about Smiley.
He may not be the biggest pet.
He may not be the fastest pet.

But he's definitely the **bravest** pet!

My sabre-tooth kitten is the best pet for
a cave-boy like me.

And I wouldn't swap him for any other pet in the world.

Talk about it!

Who is Odo, and what problem does he cause when he eats honey?

What problem did I have in the canoeing event?

What did Smiley do to earn the Bravest Pet award?

Spot the difference

Can you spot five differences between the two pictures?

Answers: One of Smiley's ears is missing, one of Fleet's ears is missing and a bit of the paw print on the Winner's Shield is missing, the paw print on the Bravest Pet trophy is missing and one bone from the necklace is missing.

Astron

Written by

John Dougherty

Illustrated by

Louise Pigott

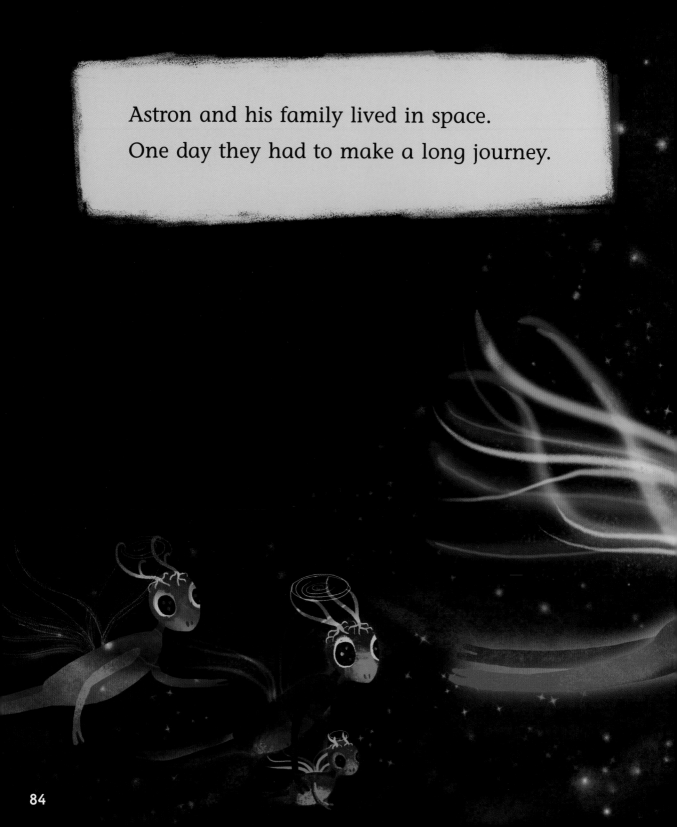

Astron and his family lived in space.
One day they had to make a long journey.

Space felt huge and cold to Astron.
He stayed close to his parents.

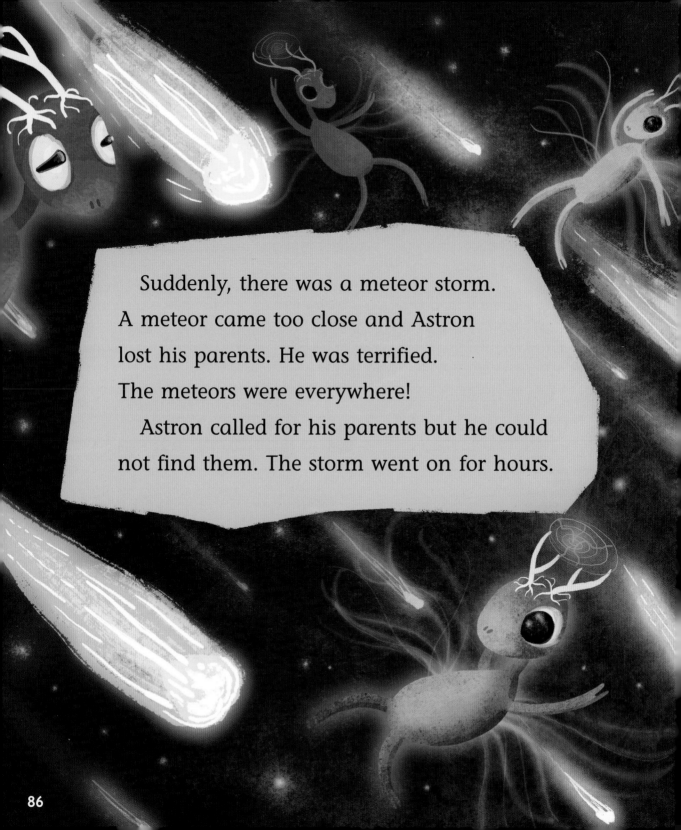

Suddenly, there was a meteor storm.
A meteor came too close and Astron
lost his parents. He was terrified.
The meteors were everywhere!

Astron called for his parents but he could
not find them. The storm went on for hours.

When the meteor storm was over, Astron
was alone. He was lost in the blackness of
space. He drifted sadly in the dark.

Then Astron saw a strange thing.
He started to fly towards it.

Astron had never seen a thing like this before. It was made of metal.

There were creatures *inside* it! He could see one of the creatures looking out.

The creature inside could see him, too.

The creature looked very strange to Astron.

It did not glow. It had no wings.

It did not even have a thought-web.

How can it talk without a thought-web?

Astron wondered.

Astron used his thought-web to listen to the creature's thoughts. Astron could tell that she was good and kind. Her name was Olivia and she was on a spaceship. She thought Astron was very strange but very beautiful.

Astron used his thought-web again. He told Olivia what he was thinking. He told her that he was lost and he needed to find his parents.

Olivia's eyes widened.

She called out to her parents. Now Astron could see how Olivia talked.

Olivia told her parents that Astron was lost. But her parents were scared of Astron and they would not listen. Olivia was cross with them.

Olivia's parents ran to the
controls of the spaceship.
They wanted to get away from
Astron as fast as possible.

The spaceship disappeared
between the stars.
Using his thought-web,
Astron felt Olivia's sadness
deep inside. He cried.

Suddenly, Astron could feel that Olivia was afraid. He listened to Olivia's thoughts. Something bad was happening to her!

Fierce creatures called dark-biters were around the spaceship.

95

The dark-biters were hungry and cruel.

They were going to eat the spaceship.

Olivia and her parents were in danger!

Astron had to save Olivia. He stretched
out his wings as **wide** as they would go.
He flew faster than he had ever flown before.
Astron hoped he would get to
Olivia in time.

Soon Astron saw the
spaceship. He was tired
but he flew even faster.

The dark-biters were nibbling
at the spaceship now.
Olivia was in great danger!
Astron went faster. He glowed **brighter**.

Then **brighter** still.

By the time Astron reached the spaceship,
he was shining with a very bright light.

The dark-biters were afraid of Astron's light.
They moved away from the spaceship.

Astron shone **brighter**
and brighter,

and the dark-biters fled.

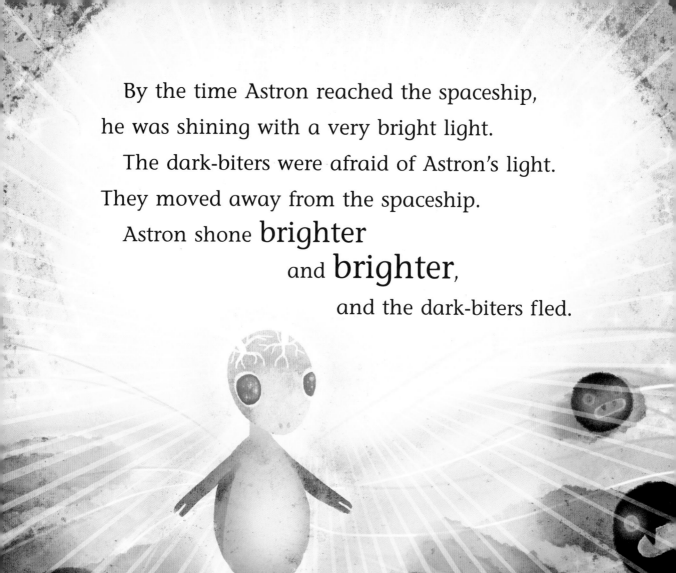

When the dark-biters had gone, Astron
had no strength left. His light began to fade.
His wings folded. Everything seemed far away.

He closed his eyes and
drifted off into space,
alone and cold.

Someone took hold of Astron.
It was Olivia's mother. She took
him into the spaceship.

Olivia was upset. "We have to help him!" she cried. "We will help him," said Olivia's father. "I'm sorry we were afraid of him."

Olivia's mother said, "Maybe we can find out where his family is. Let's use the computer to look."

After a while, the computer beeped. Had it found Astron's family?

The spaceship flew towards the signal.

Soon, Astron could hear his family's thoughts. He felt a warm glow of happiness as he got closer to his family.

Olivia opened the spaceship door. She cried as she said goodbye to Astron.

Astron cried, too. He might never see Olivia again but he knew they would always be friends.

Astron flew through the door and went to join his parents.

As the spaceship flew away, Astron
saw Olivia waving. He stretched out his
wings and waved back.

The spaceship vanished
among the stars.
Even when Olivia was far away, Astron
could still feel her thoughts inside his head.

Talk about it!

What was Astron trying to find?

Can you think of three ways in which Astron and I are different?

How did my parents feel about Astron at first? Why did they change their minds?

Choose the right words

Read the sentences. Write the correct word in each gap.

1. Astron was _____ in space.
   (happy, lost, ill)

2. Olivia wanted to _____ Astron.
   (help, ignore, avoid)

3. Astron _____ the dark-biters with
   his light. (entertained, helped, scared)

4. Olivia's _____ came to rescue
   Astron. (cat, mother, father)

Answers:
1. lost;
2. help;
3. scared;
4. mother

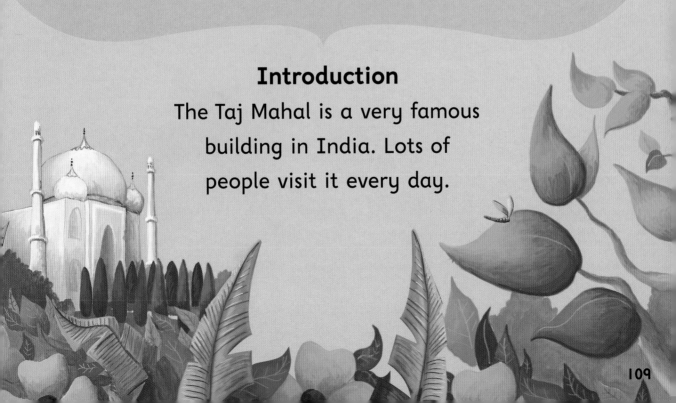

The Top of the Taj Mahal

Written by Narinder Dhami

Illustrated by Anaïs Goldemberg

Introduction

The Taj Mahal is a very famous building in India. Lots of people visit it every day.

Mishu the little monkey had ten brothers and sisters.

They lived with their mum and dad
in the gardens of the Taj Mahal.

Mishu thought the Taj Mahal was amazing. He loved the big white dome, the four tall towers and the beautiful pool.

The pool had fountains! Mishu loved to run past the fountains as they shot up into the air.

One day, Mishu's brothers and sisters
were playing hide-and-seek in the trees.
"Can I play?" asked Mishu.

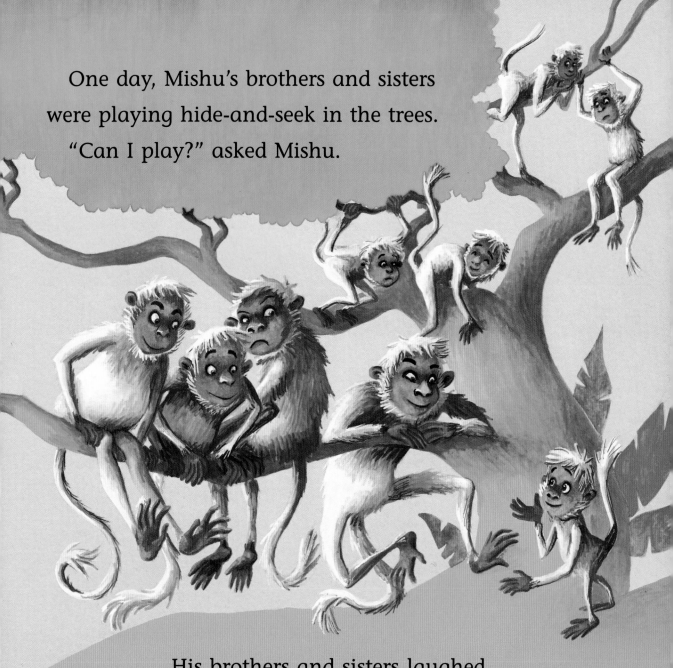

His brothers and sisters laughed.
"You can't climb as high as we can,"
they said. "You're too *small!*"

Mishu stared sadly at his brothers and sisters.
They never let him join in with their games.

"I can climb higher than
all of you!" boasted Mishu.
"And I'm going to climb to
the top of the Taj Mahal!"

"You are a silly little monkey. The Taj Mahal is too big to climb!" said Mishu's brothers and sisters.

And they left, swinging from tree to tree.

Mishu went to find his best friend, Kojo the parakeet.

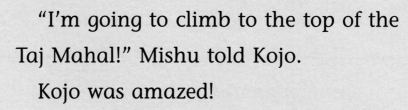

"I'm going to climb to the top of the
Taj Mahal!" Mishu told Kojo.
Kojo was amazed!

"But the Taj Mahal is as high as
the sun in the sky!" she squawked.

"I'm still going to try," Mishu said.
"Will you come with me?"

Kojo flapped her wings. "Of course I will," she replied.

Let's go!

So Mishu and Kojo set off through the gardens to the Taj Mahal.

"Are you off to climb the Taj Mahal, Mishu?" his sisters teased.

"You need wings, like Kojo," shouted his brothers.
"Then you can *fly* to the top!"
And they all burst out laughing.

"I'll show *you!*"
Mishu cried.

The Taj Mahal was closed that day. The fountains
had been turned off and the pool was clear and still.

Mishu could see the reflection
of the Taj Mahal in the water.

Mishu and Kojo went up to the
Taj Mahal. It was taller than the tallest
tree in the gardens. It looked bigger
and bigger as they got closer and closer.

Suddenly Mishu felt very small and scared.
He took a deep breath ...

Mishu tried to jump on to the wall
of the Taj Mahal. But the white stone
was very smooth and very shiny,
so Mishu just slid down the wall.

"Try again, Mishu," Kojo called. "But be careful."

Mishu tried again. And again. But every time, he slid back down.

"You're a brave monkey, Mishu," said Kojo. "But the wall is too smooth and shiny to climb."

"I need another plan," said Mishu.

Mishu sat down and thought for a while.

"I've got it!" cried Mishu. "Kojo, will you fly me to the top of the Taj Mahal?"

"Of course!" Kojo replied. "Grab on to my legs and don't let go!"

Mishu held on to Kojo's legs with his paws.
At last, he was going to the top of the Taj Mahal!

Kojo flapped her wings but she and Mishu didn't
fly up into the air. Kojo flapped her wings harder
and harder but nothing happened.

Finally, Kojo gave up.

"You're too heavy for me, Mishu!" Kojo panted.

"Thank you for trying to help," Mishu said sadly.

"I'll never get to the top of the Taj Mahal now!"
sighed Mishu.

Mishu and Kojo walked home in silence.

On the way, they passed the pool.

Mishu noticed the reflection of the Taj Mahal in the water again. This time, it gave him a wonderful idea!

"Kojo, will you go and find my brothers
and sisters?" Mishu asked. "Tell them
I'm on top of the Taj Mahal!"

Kojo looked puzzled. "But you're *not!*" she squawked.
"Just go and tell them!" laughed Mishu.

Kojo didn't know what Mishu was up to. But she flew off and found Mishu's brothers and sisters playing in the trees.

"Come quickly," Kojo called.
"Mishu is on top of the Taj Mahal!"

"He *can't* be!" the monkeys gasped.

The monkeys followed Kojo to the pool.
Mishu was standing on one of the fountains.

"Look at me!" Mishu yelled. "I'm on top of
the Taj Mahal!"

But Mishu's brothers and sisters just looked
very confused.

"But you're *not* on top of the Taj Mahal!"
said one of Mishu's brothers.

"Oh yes, I am!" said Mishu, grinning.
"Look at the water!"

The fountain was right on top of the reflection
of the Taj Mahal!

Everyone began to laugh.

"What a clever little monkey you are, Mishu," said his brothers and sisters. "You and Kojo can join in with our games from now on!"

"No," Mishu laughed. "You can join in with *our* games!"

Talk about it!

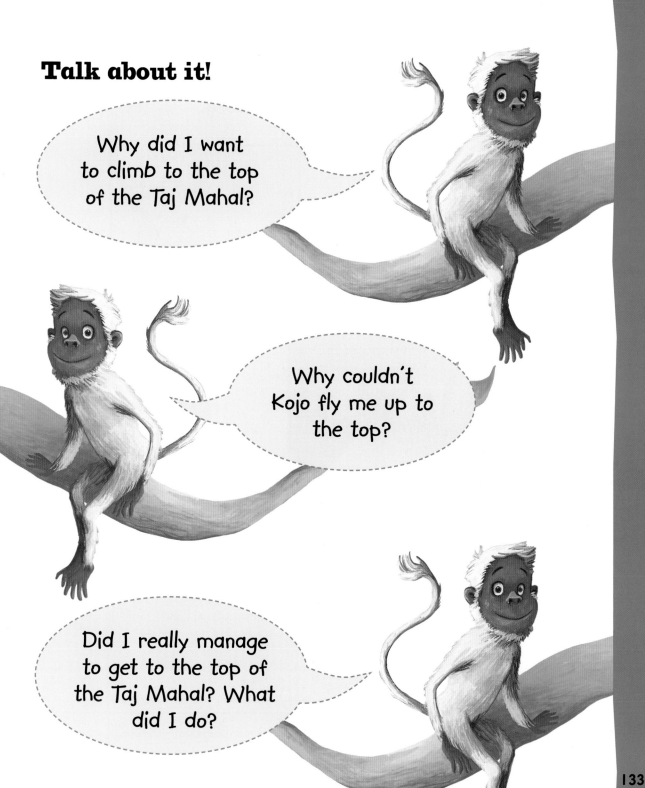

Why did I want to climb to the top of the Taj Mahal?

Why couldn't Kojo fly me up to the top?

Did I really manage to get to the top of the Taj Mahal? What did I do?

133

Retell the story

Use the pictures to help you retell the story.

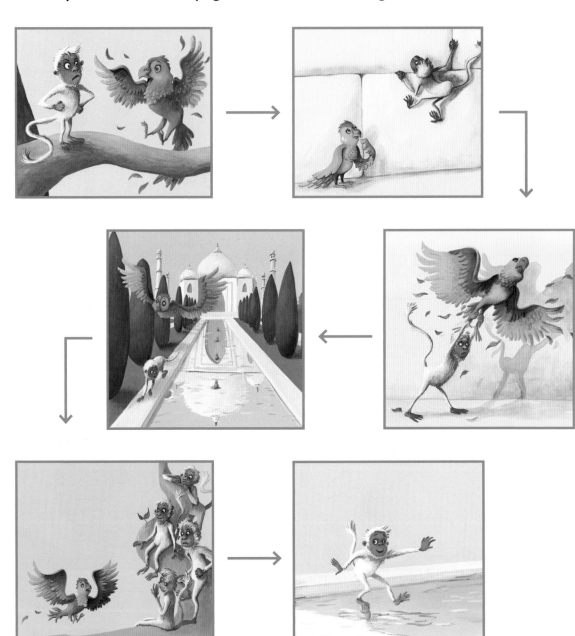

Plughole

Written by **Geoff Havel**

Illustrated by **Shane McGowan**

Glug,

glug,

glug,

Down the plug.

Where does the water go?

Imagine if ...

There's a monster living underground,
Who drinks bathwater from all around.

That poor monster, all alone,
Sits upon his lonely throne.
And when you listen, when you peek,
You hear the monster's lonely squeak.

He's all alone and he wonders when
He might be able to find a friend.

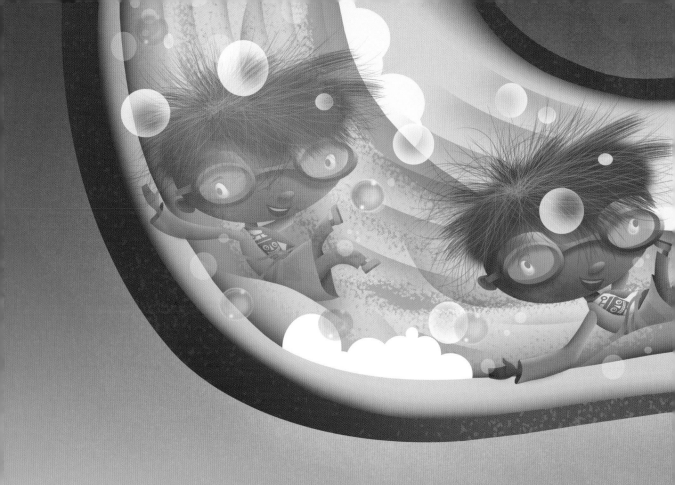

And imagine if ...

One night before you go to sleep,
Into a nice warm bath you leap.
Once you're clean from toes to chin,
You pull the plug and dive right in!

Round and round and round you go,
Sometimes fast and sometimes slow.

All along the pipe you zoom,
Into the monster's soapy room.

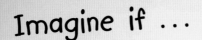

Imagine if ...

The monster has been getting thinner
And so you kindly cook his dinner.
His favourite meal, all slimy and green.
The yuckiest stuff you've ever seen!

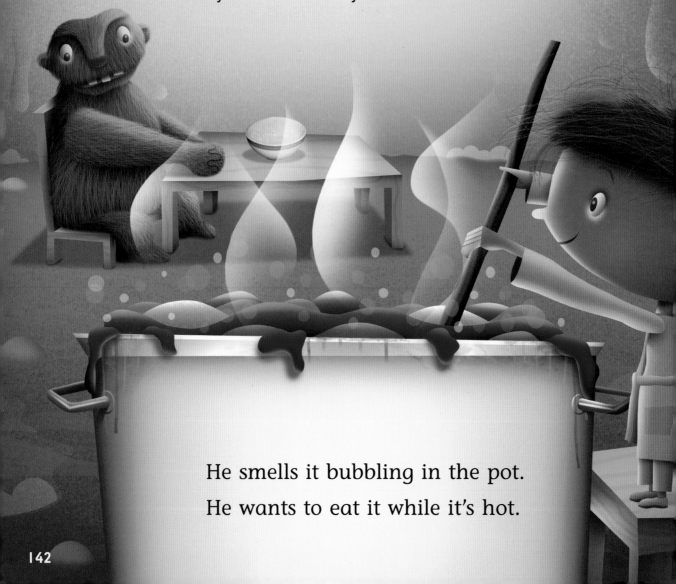

He smells it bubbling in the pot.
He wants to eat it while it's hot.

"Dinner's ready!" you say with a grin.
You take his bowl and pour some in.
It's grey and green with patches of brown
But the monster gurgles and guzzles it down.

143

And imagine if ...

Soon it's time for you to go,

But the lonely monster just says, "No!"

When you try to rush away,

The lonely monster wants to play.

But soon the playtime has to end.
The monster needs another friend …
You choose a friend to make him smile –
A plastic duck with lots of style!

To get that duck you'll have to crawl
Back up the pipe that's in the wall.
And when you take another peep,
You can see it's very steep.

Imagine if ...

Now your brother must get clean,
In the bubbliest bath that's ever been.
He uses lots of the bubbly stuff –
A tiny drop should be enough!

Lots of bubbles – more and more!
Frothy bubbles pour onto the floor!

So then your mum pulls out the plug,

Glug, glug, glug, glug, glug, glug, glug.

The monster says, "Yum, yum, yum, yummy!"
And guzzles the bubbles into his tummy.

Imagine if ...

The bubbles **pop** inside his belly.
He starts to **shake** like a bowl of jelly.

He opens his mouth and you see inside ...

And he blows a bubble a metre wide!

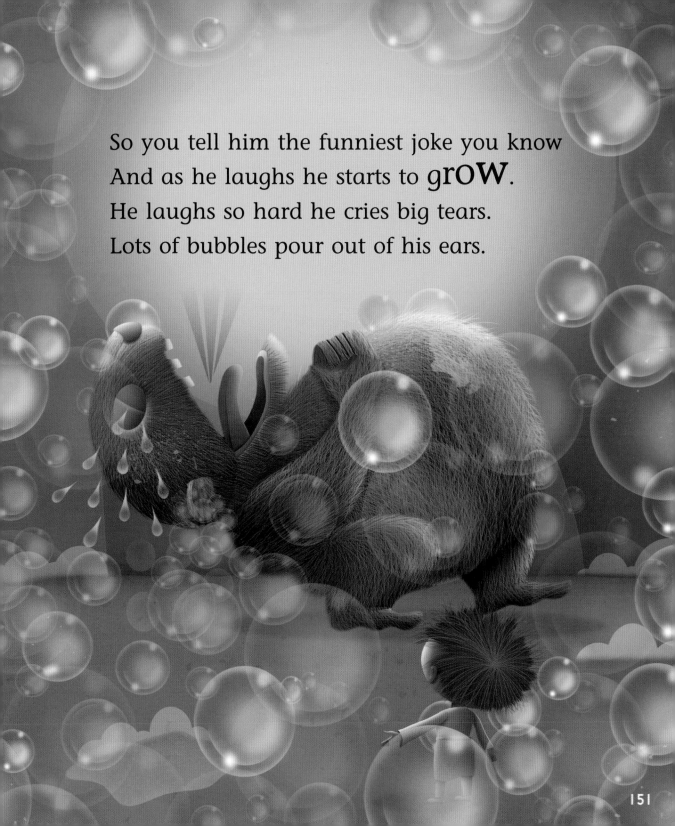

So you tell him the funniest joke you know
And as he laughs he starts to gr**OW**.
He laughs so hard he cries big tears.
Lots of bubbles pour out of his ears.

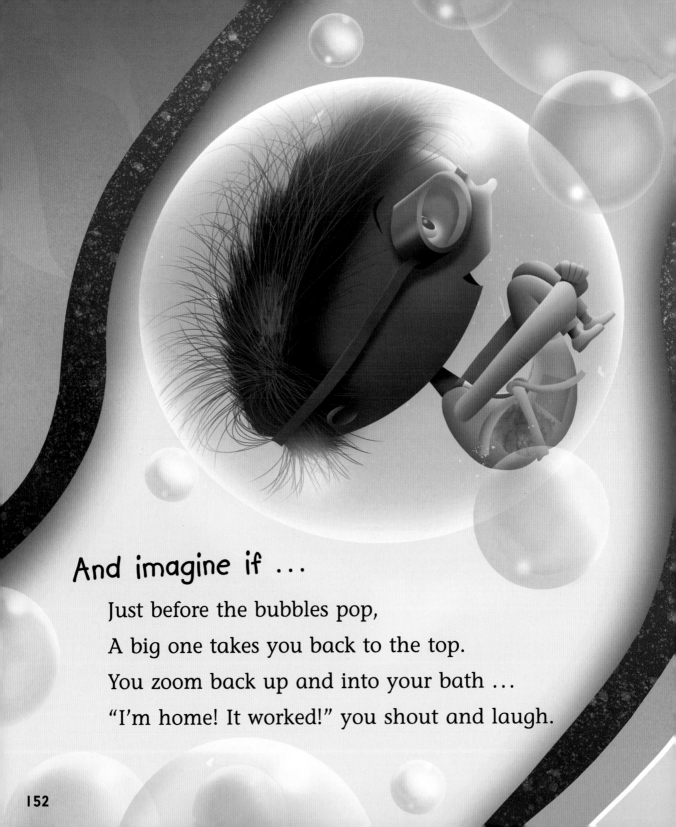

And imagine if …

Just before the bubbles pop,

A big one takes you back to the top.

You zoom back up and into your bath …

"I'm home! It worked!" you shout and laugh.

But from the plughole you hear a mumble,
A gurgling, slurping …

… giant **rumble!**

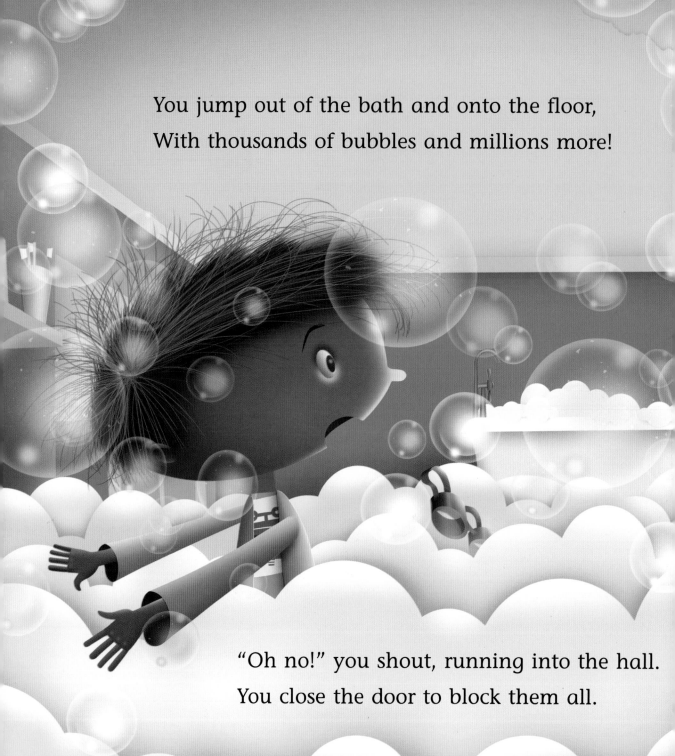

You jump out of the bath and onto the floor,
With thousands of bubbles and millions more!

"Oh no!" you shout, running into the hall.
You close the door to block them all.

Imagine if ...

Your mum comes when she hears you shout.

She runs to see what the noise is about.

She says to you, "Your bath took a while!"

"Did it?" you ask with a cheeky smile.

Imagine if ...

Next time you have a bubbly bath,
You think of the monster and start to laugh.
Is he still down there all by himself?
You grab your plastic duck from the shelf!

You pull the plug and then you send
The lonely monster a duck for a friend.

157

Talk about it!

What did I cook for the monster?

What did I send down to be the monster's friend?

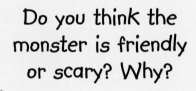

Do you think the monster is friendly or scary? Why?

Plughole word search

Can you find these words from the story in the word search grid?

c	n	r	g	w	m	y	s
p	l	u	g	h	o	l	e
a	z	m	d	q	n	e	l
o	d	b	u	h	s	n	b
s	p	l	c	y	t	o	b
b	u	e	k	v	e	l	u
d	i	n	n	e	r	x	b
f	j	d	n	e	i	r	f

plughole   monster   soap

bubbles   duck   lonely

dinner   rumble   friend

OXFORD

UNIVERSITY PRESS

Great Clarendon Street, Oxford, OX2 6DP, United Kingdom

Oxford University Press is a department of the University
of Oxford. It furthers the University's objective of excellence
in research, scholarship, and education by publishing worldwide.
Oxford is a registered trade mark of Oxford University Press
in the UK and in certain other countries

British Library Cataloguing in Publication Data

Data available

ISBN: 978-0-19-277381-4

10 9 8 7 6 5 4 3 2 1

Paper used in the production of this book is a natural, recyclable product
made from wood grown in sustainable forests. The manufacturing process
conforms to the environmental regulations of the country of origin.

Printed in China

Acknowledgements

Series Advisor: Nikki Gamble